JASON ALEXANDER

DAD, ARE YOU THE TOOTH FAIRY?

Illustrated by **RON SPEARS**

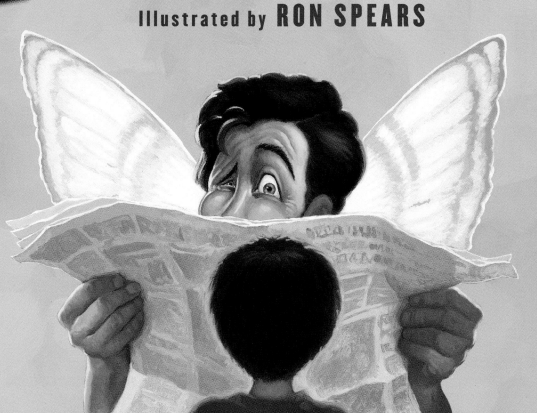

ORCHARD BOOKS · AN IMPRINT OF SCHOLASTIC INC. · NEW YORK

I dedicate this book to my sons, Gabriel and Noah, who bring magic and endless possibilities to my life every day. And to their mother, my wife Daena, whose boundless love and energy make all three of her men the best human beings we can be.

And lastly, for the young readers or listeners to this story,
every single word of it is absolutely true . . . if you believe.

—J. A.

To Karen, George, Sandra, and Staci

—R. S.

Text copyright © 2005 by Jason Alexander
Illustrations copyright © 2005 by Ron Spears

Library of Congress Cataloging-in-Publication Data available
ISBN: 0-439-66745-3

10 9 8 7 6 5 4 3 2   05 06 07 08 09
Printed in Singapore   46
First edition, May 2005

Gaby had a loose tooth. But Gaby didn't mind, for he had had loose teeth before. In fact, he *liked* loose teeth.

Gaby did the same thing with every tooth that fell out. He put it in a special envelope his parents always gave him. At bedtime, it went under his pillow. When he woke up the next morning, he found the envelope had a message written on it, and each time it was signed by someone named Gwyneth.

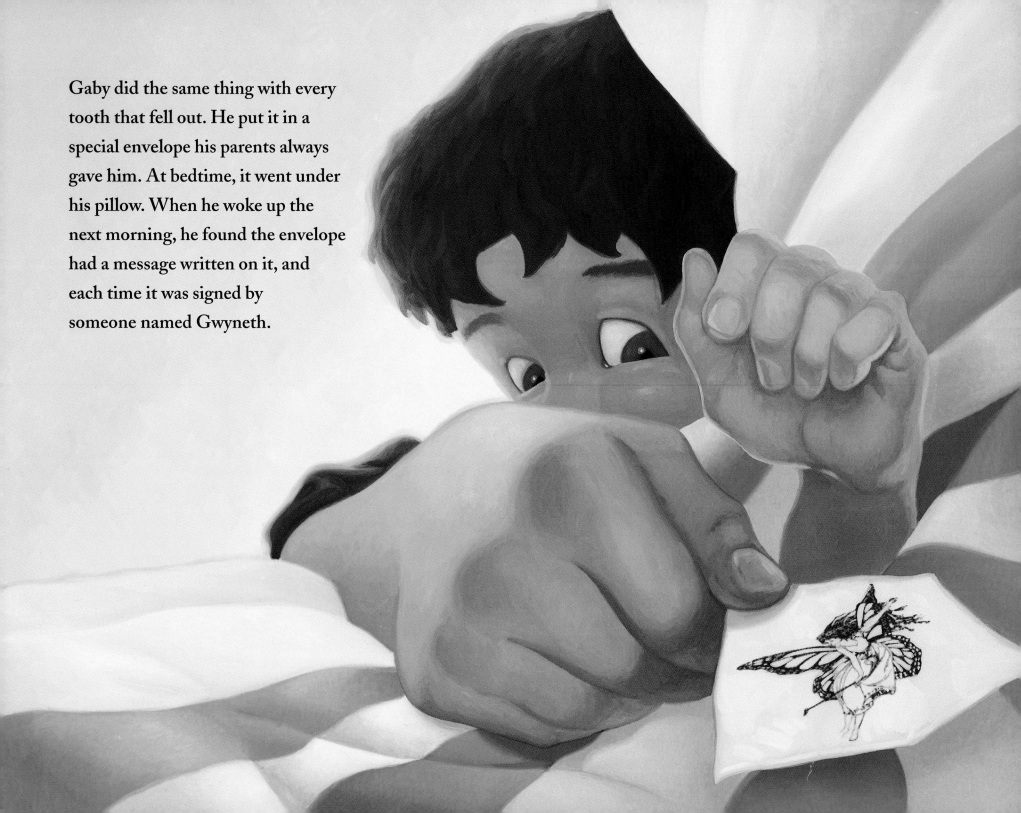

Gwyneth wrote that she was Gaby's personal tooth fairy. She thanked him for his baby tooth and wrote how lovely she thought his new tooth would be. She often wrote about her world, and how the other fairies wished that the teeth in their collections were as wonderful as hers. And always she told Gaby what a special boy he was.

Gaby liked his fairy's notes and loved what she left
inside each envelope. His baby tooth was always
gone, and in its place would be a gift: two coins.
A whole silver dollar and a new, shiny penny. The
dollar for the old tooth, the penny for the new.

And so it had gone, year after year, tooth after tooth.

Till one day Gaby was not a little boy anymore. He was a bigger boy, and bigger boys, like bigger girls, sometimes overhear things they'd rather not have heard.

Gaby heard from older kids that sorcerers and superheroes simply weren't real. He heard there never was a genie trapped inside a lamp. And certainly no Goldilocks, Cinderella, Sleeping Beauty, Rumpelstiltskin, Hansel, Gretel, Snow White, Jack, or beanstalk. And by the way, the Easter Bunny was highly doubtful, too.

Gaby also heard (and I'm sad to say he listened) that tooth fairies were nothing more than childish make-believe. That it was really moms and dads who tiptoed into children's rooms, threw away the old teeth, and left gifts behind.

Gaby was confused. Would his friends try to fool him? Would his *parents*? How could anyone know what was truly true?

To make things worse, Gaby had this new loose tooth! Well, now he simply *had* to know for sure. So bravely he went up and asked his dad this very big question. "Dad, I need the absolutely total honest truth. Is there really a tooth fairy named Gwyneth who comes and takes my teeth? Or is it only you and Mom . . . for *real*?"

Gaby's dad sat and took a slow, deep breath. "Okay, pal, I'll try to give a truly honest answer," he said. "The only honest answer I can give."

Once, long ago, all kinds of creatures roamed the earth. There were dinosaurs and mastodons and dodo birds and such. But, as you know, today they are all gone.

Long ago there were also magical creatures — everything from unicorns to minotaurs and mermaids to dragons, wizards, trolls, and elves. And most of all there were fairies.

There were fairies by the thousands —
hundreds of thousands — maybe more.
Twinkling balls of light and sparkle, flitting
about the world. Creatures made of stardust,
whispers, memories, and mist.

Well, years passed, and many people turned away from magic. For what they really wanted was to control the world themselves. So they learned the wizards' tricks for turning nighttime into day. They learned to change the weather, the oceans, and the land. But the more they controlled the world, the more the magic faded.

And so, too, the creatures of magic also started to fade. First the dragons, then the unicorns. Then one by one the wizards, the elves, and all the others.

The last to go were the fairies. Where they went, no one knows. For it is said — and I believe — that magical creatures cannot die. Some say the fairies went to uncharted islands. Some say they went to the stars, others to the moon. All we know for sure is they're certainly not here.

And as the fairies disappeared, the children were filled with sadness. They missed their fairy gifts. But more, they missed their fairy friends.

So seeing their tears, the final little fairy stopped and made a promise to the children of the world before she left. "From this day forth," she said, "you shall not see another fairy. So much has changed, and so few people believe in us anymore. But if you try — if you really try — our voices may still be heard."

"From this day forth, your parents must take the teeth from beneath your pillows. Then they will sit in a quiet place with a pencil in their hands. They'll close their eyes and soon they'll hear a voice inside their heads."

"The voice will tell them what to write and what treasures to exchange. And as long as their children believe in this magic, then so long will we fairies keep speaking. And you shall have our words and our little gifts of love."

*T*hen one child sweetly asked, "How will our parents truly know if the voice inside their heads comes from you or from themselves?"

"They won't know," said the fairy. "And neither then will you. You must trust that it is us, or we truly shall be gone." And with that the final fairy ever to be seen — vanished.

"The true and honest answer to your question," said Gaby's dad, "is that *I* take the envelope from under your pillow while you sleep. *I* sit in a quiet place with my pencil in my hand. And when I hear the voice inside my head, *I* write the words."

Then, Dad went on, "But I think the thing you're really asking is: Is the voice I hear my own, or is it something else? A voice, perhaps, belonging to a fairy named Gwyneth? The answer to that question, Gaby, cannot come from me. *That* answer has to come from you and you alone."

Gaby thought and thought, and then finally he said, "I just don't know, Dad, what the truthful answer is. But I'm going to believe that the voice is a fairy named Gwyneth and that she is somehow mine, and I am somehow hers. And I hope that she's alive and well in some magical place." Then Gaby smiled a loose-tooth smile. And Dad smiled back. They were smiles that meant a lot of things, but mostly meant "I love you."

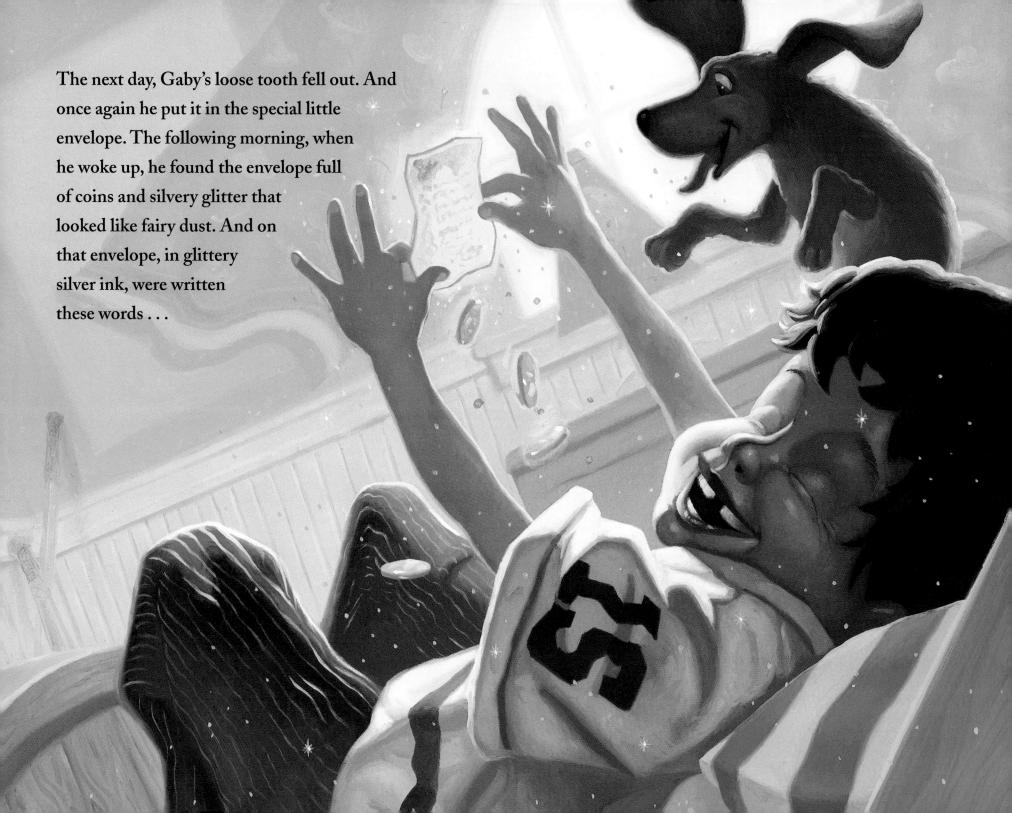

The next day, Gaby's loose tooth fell out. And once again he put it in the special little envelope. The following morning, when he woke up, he found the envelope full of coins and silvery glitter that looked like fairy dust. And on that envelope, in glittery silver ink, were written these words . . .

Dearest Gaby,

I have given you many gifts. But you have given yourself the greatest gift of all — possibilities. May magic fill your life. Your world will never be ordinary, for you have chosen to live by your heart. Your mind will keep you safe. Your heart will keep you happy. I am proud to be your friend and prouder to be your tooth fairy. Joy to you always.

Love,
Gwyneth

P. S. Say hello to your dad.

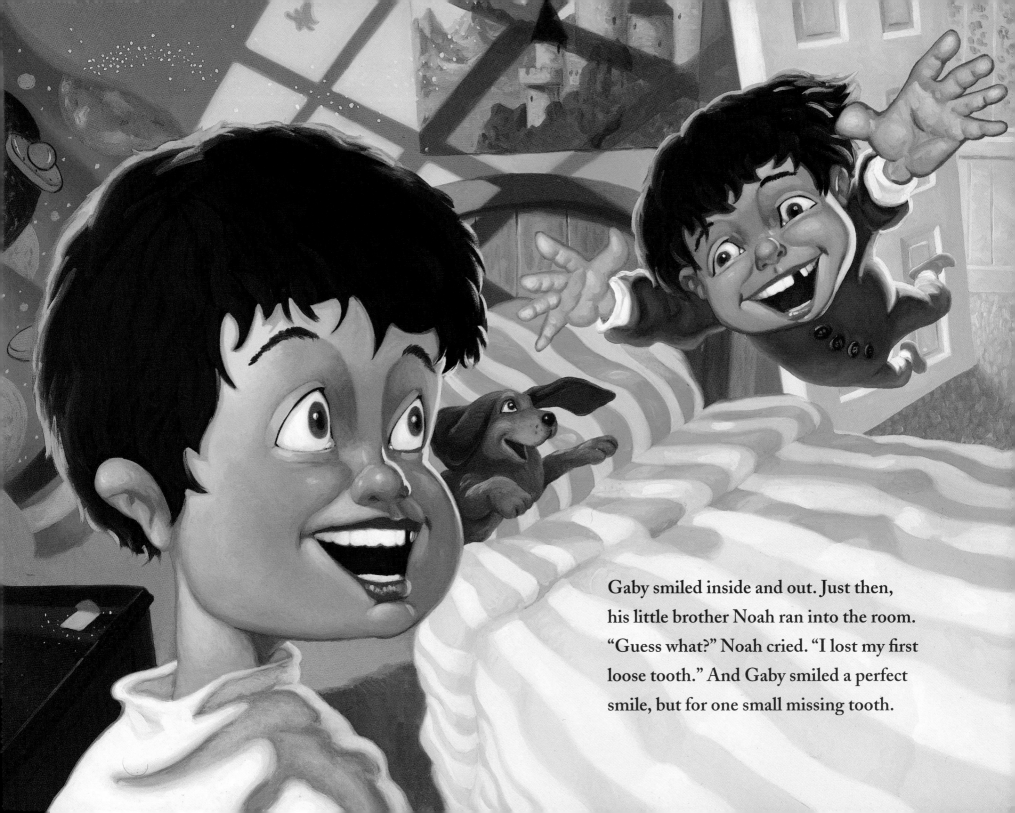

Gaby smiled inside and out. Just then, his little brother Noah ran into the room. "Guess what?" Noah cried. "I lost my first loose tooth." And Gaby smiled a perfect smile, but for one small missing tooth.

A NOTE FROM THE AUTHOR

This story is, more or less, an actual conversation I had with my son Gabriel some years ago. It is not a story intended solely for children. Rather it is an example of the magic that can happen when parents have a good day. My son wanted the truth, but he clearly didn't want something precious taken from him. I was happily able to give him both. Some parents may feel I did him a disservice. And I accept that part of our parental responsibility is to prepare our children for the harshest of realities. But as Gwyneth says, it needs to be a balance between their heads and their hearts. One without the other is an empty life. And ultimately, I believe if you care for their hearts, their heads will be just fine. If this story inspires you to have a good parent day, then I am deeply gratified.

THE TOOTH FAIRY ENVELOPE DEPICTED IN THE BOOK IS A REPLICA OF THE ONE MY FAMILY ACTUALLY USES. THEY WERE CREATED BY MY FRIEND, GREG LENERT. YOU MAY ORDER THEM AT WWW.TOOTHFAIRYENVELOPES.COM.